Welcome to Percy's Park!

Percy the park keeper
works hard looking after
the park and his animal
friends who live there.
But Percy still likes to
find time for some fun
and games. And, of
course, in Percy's Park,
there's always time
for a story...

One Springy Day

Cleo…
Have I told you recently?
I like you!

This book is for you,
With heaps of love from
Grandpa

First published in hardback in Great Britain by HarperCollins Children's Books in 2019

5 7 9 10 8 6 4

ISBN: 978-0-00-827986-8

Text and illustrations copyright © Nick Butterworth 2019

HarperCollins Children's Books is a division of HarperCollins Publishers Ltd.

Visit our website at: www.harpercollins.co.uk

Printed and bound in China

Nick Butterworth

One Springy Day

HarperCollins *Children's Books*

"Ninety-seven, ninety-eight, ninety-nine," Percy the park keeper counted. "One hundred! Coming, ready or not!"

Percy's animal friends were ready. All, except one.

"Oh dear," said the fox. "Where shall I hide?"

"I can see you, hedgehog," Percy called. "Found you!"

The fox stood by the door to Percy's workshop.

"Oh dear. Percy said not to go in here, but…but…"

Percy called again. He was getting closer.

"Three rabbits in my wheelbarrow. Found you!"

This was too much for the fox.
He put his paws over his ears and
slipped through the workshop
doorway.

"There must be somewhere
to hide in here," he
muttered. He stopped
by some tall shelves
and looked up.
"I wonder…"

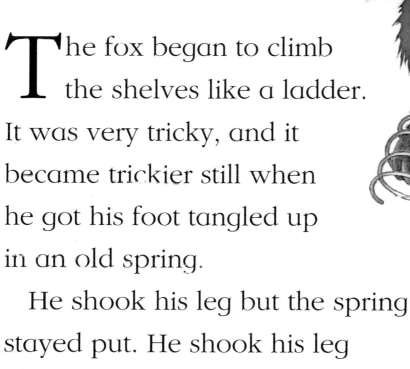

The fox began to climb the shelves like a ladder. It was very tricky, and it became trickier still when he got his foot tangled up in an old spring.

He shook his leg but the spring stayed put. He shook his leg harder and harder. The shelves began to sway.

"Get off," the fox moaned, "Percy's coming. I need to…

…ooooooooooooh!"

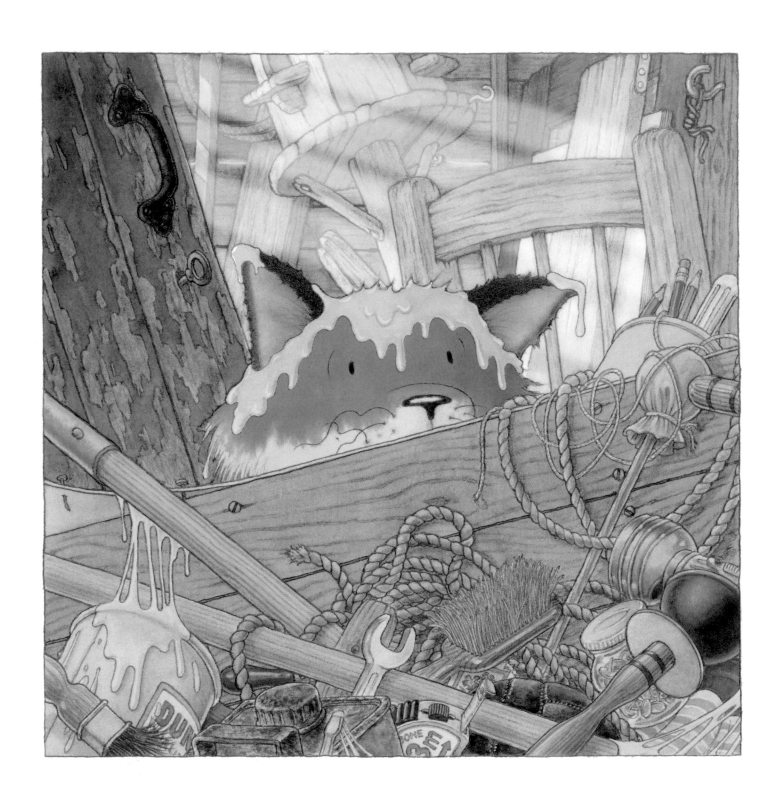

CRRR-ASH!
The shelves tipped forward and emptied everything on them, including the fox, onto the floor.

The fox wasn't hurt. But something wasn't right. He felt sticky. Very, very sticky.

"What was that noise?!" said a voice outside.

"Oh no! It's Percy!" The fox jumped to his feet and bundled himself into a nearby cupboard. Just in time.

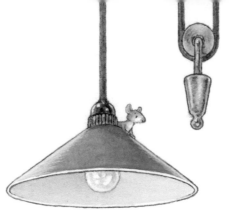

"Is somebody in here?"

Percy walked into the workshop, followed by all the other animals. He looked at the fallen shelves.

"Oh my goodness! What a mess! Everything's covered in my Very Sticky Glue."

"Look!" said the hedgehog. He pointed to a line of footprints across the floor leading to the cupboard where Percy kept things he needed for his work.

S lowly, Percy opened the cupboard door. There was no sign of the fox.

"Fox," Percy called softly. "Are you in there?"

There was a pause.

"No," said the fox. The animals giggled together.

"Then who can it be?" said Percy.

"Don't know," said the fox.

"It's definitely not me."

Percy chuckled. "Come on.

Out you come."

To everyone's amazement, not only did the fox step out of the cupboard, but so did everything else! All at once. All stuck together!

"Woah!" said Percy.

The animals began to laugh. They laughed and laughed. Only the fox didn't think it was funny. With one foot still stuck in the troublesome spring and the other in a paint pot, he ran from the workshop.

Clomp...boing...clomp...boing...clomp...boing...

"Fox!" called Percy. "Come back!"
The animals looked at each other.
"Oh dear," said Percy. "I think
he's upset."

O utside, the fox was nowhere to be seen.
"We need a search party," said the owl…

"No need for that. Look there!" said a squirrel.
"It's a trail of clues left by the fox!"

"Well done," said Percy.

"Listen!" said one of the rabbits. Everyone stood
quite still…

…clomp…boing…clomp…boing…clomp…boing…

"Aha!" said Percy. "We'll soon find him.
And remember, when we do,
no laughing!"

W ith the rabbits racing ahead, Percy and his friends followed the trail, collecting up all the clues in Percy's wheelbarrow.

"Phew! I need a breather."

Percy sat down on the roots of an ancient hollow tree. Two rabbits ran up to him.

"The trail has run out. We can't find any more clues."

"That's a nuisance," said Percy. "It'll be harder to find the fox now. He could be…"

Boing…

Percy stopped. The *boingy* sound seemed to come from inside the tree. Percy smiled and signalled for everyone to keep quiet.

"Hello, fox," he said. There was no reply.

Percy went on. "Would you like to come out now?"

"Can't," said the fox. "Stuck."

Everyone tried very hard not to laugh.

"Let's give you a hand then," said Percy.

He reached into the hollow tree and found, not the fox, but the handle of a bucket. He gave a tug.

"Goodness! You really are stuck. Right. Come on, everyone. This calls for some team work!"

Percy and the animals tied ropes and strings to the bucket handle and other bits and pieces that were stuck to the fox's fur. They tugged and they pulled, again and again, but still, the stuck fox stayed stuck.

The badger whispered to Percy.
"I think it's his bottom?"
"His bottom?" said Percy. "What's the matter
with his bottom?"
"It's stuck to the tree," said the badger.

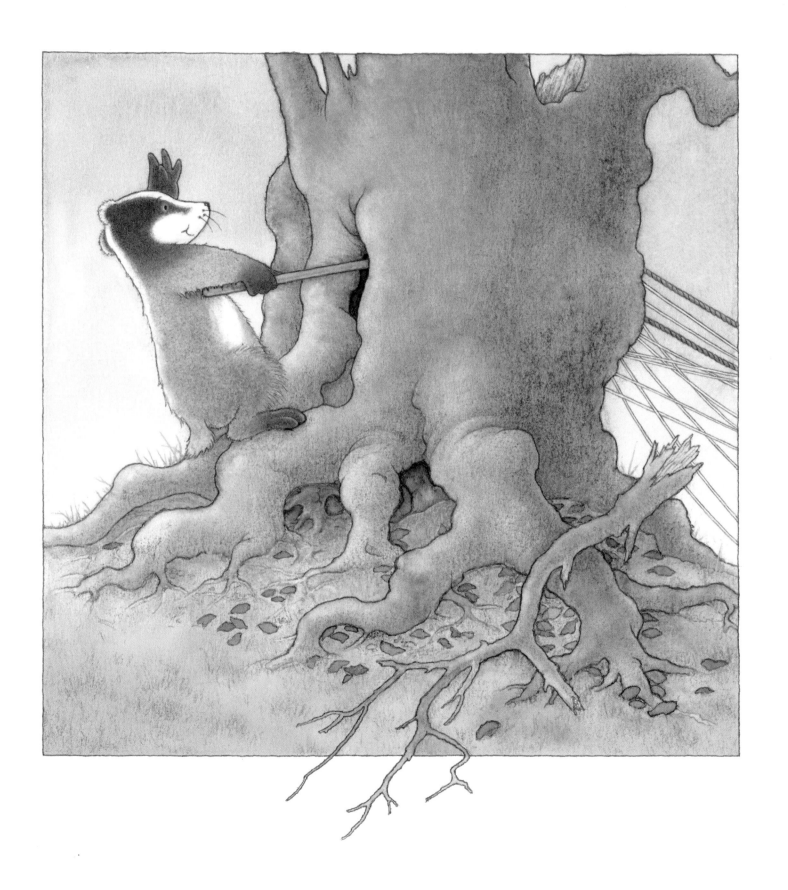

The badger picked up a mop from Percy's wheelbarrow and went to the other side of the tree.

"I've got an idea," he said. "When I say 'Go!' give it one more heave."

The badger gently pushed the mop through a split in the tree trunk.

"What's that?" said a muffled voice.

"Who's poking my...?"

"Take the strain," called Percy.

"Ready badger?"

"GO!" shouted the badger.

"Not for me, thanks," said the fox.
"I've had enough sticky stuff for one day."
Percy chuckled. "Never mind," he said.
"Tomorrow will be another fine spring day."
"Please," said the fox, "don't mention springs!"